Grief Hotel

by Liza Birkenmeier

song by Jordan McCree
and Liza Birkenmeier

No one shall make any changes in this title(s) for the purpose of production. No part of this book may be reproduced, stored in a retrieval system, scanned, uploaded, or transmitted in any form, by any means, now known or yet to be invented, including mechanical, electronic, digital, photocopying, recording, videotaping, or otherwise, without the prior written permission of the publisher. No one shall share this title(s), or any part of this title(s), through any social media or file hosting websites.

For all inquiries regarding motion picture, television, online/digital and other media rights, please contact Concord Theatricals Corp.

MUSIC AND THIRD-PARTY MATERIALS USE NOTE

Licensees are solely responsible for obtaining formal written permission from copyright owners to use copyrighted music and/or other copyrighted third-party materials (e.g. artworks, logos) in the performance of this play and are strongly cautioned to do so. If no such permission is obtained by the licensee, then the licensee must use only original music and materials that the licensee owns and controls. Licensees are solely responsible and liable for clearances of all third-party copyrighted materials, including without limitation music, and shall indemnify the copyright owners of the play(s) and their licensing agent, Concord Theatricals Corp., against any costs, expenses, losses and liabilities arising from the use of such copyrighted third-party materials by licensees. For music, please contact the appropriate music licensing authority in your territory for the rights to any incidental music.

IMPORTANT BILLING AND CREDIT REQUIREMENTS

If you have obtained performance rights to this title, please refer to your licensing agreement for important billing and credit requirements.

GRIEF HOTEL premiered with Clubbed Thumb as part of Summerworks at the Wild Project in June 2023. It was remounted with Clubbed Thumb and New Georges at The Public Theatre in April 2024 with the same cast and creative team. Both productions were directed by Tara Ahmadinejad, with sound design and original compositions by Jordan McCree, set design by dots, costume design by Mel Ng, and lighting design by Masha Tsimring. The Production Stage Manager was Allison Raynes. The cast was as follows:

AUNT BOBBI . . . . Susan Blommaert

EM . . . . Nadine Malouf

WINN . . . . Ana Nogueira

TERESA . . . . Susannah Perkins

ROHIT . . . . Naren Weiss

ASHER . . . . Bruce McKenzie

CHARACTERS

AUNT BOBBI – a force

EM – ceremoniously agitated, thirties

WINN – sadly impulsive, same age as Em

TERESA – unnervingly self-satisfied, a little younger than Em and Winn

ROHIT – uncertain but so deliberate, same age as Em and Winn

ASHER – used to be famous, twenty to thirty years older than Winn

AUTHOR'S NOTES

a note on set:

not enough furniture

maybe they look like they're in a hotel conference room or lobby, but maybe not

maybe a "musical chairs" quality arises and falls now and again, but maybe not

maybe once they enter, they can't leave (except for Asher)

otherwise:

there aren't any objects until the end

(**AUNT BOBBI** *proudly shows us an invisible thing.*)

(*Meanwhile,* **WINN** *and* **ASHER** *are somewhere, not looking at each other, not looking at* **AUNT BOBBI**.)

(*They are texting, but don't have phones. Their speech might be overconfident, aspirational; maybe they sound how they wish they would.*)

(*These two things are not happening at the same time or in the same place.*)

AUNT BOBBI. My creative expression was a picture book about your hotel chain because that was one of the choices on the assignment sheet. I picked this, ah, picture book, to talk about an idea of how you can get young people to go to your hotel. I didn't put a title on it. So here's the first part, which, this is the part where there is a girl named Penelope. This is when she drops her baby on her head. I thought the name Penelope was hilarious. So then here is where Penelope finds out that her baby has irreversible brain damage. This is pediatric intensive care. The baby doesn't have a name.

    ASHER. Hi. It's John from Tinder. I can send you pics.

    WINN. Hey, John. I think I was chatting with you on OkCupid.

    ASHER. Yeah that's right. That's embarrassing.

    WINN. It's really not. I just wanted to be sure you hadn't mistaken me for someone else.

ASHER. Recently got on all the apps at once. I can't keep it all straight.

WINN. Meeting lots of people?

ASHER. There's no good answer to that, is there?

AUNT BOBBI. Well then here's a picture of Penelope coming home from the hospital and thinking about taking an entire bottle of a serious prescription medication because how is she going to live with herself. Oh but first her husband divorces her, but – that's this page, but – let's interject and imagine he was just some good-for-nothing a-hole, and we're not worried about him. So Penelope is single and has this brain-damaged baby and she's not sure how she's going to keep living her life, because her baby is going to grow up with a million problems that are just muy muy expensive and she's thinking: well, I could be better off dead. So these are her friends hanging out and drinking wine because the... I think that's what some girls do so. They're pretty worried about Penelope so here they go googling some stuff they wanna get her. Little uh. Stuff. They, here – this – just don't know what to get Penelope: some question marks. So but then – so here they're drinking wine and looking at computers – they think might as well get her a *trip*. Here's Penelope starving herself in front of a television that isn't even on.

    ASHER. Can I be straightforward and ask you a question? Maybe it's none of my business, but I think it's important.

WINN. Exciting. Yes.

    (**ASHER** *is so serious.*)

ASHER. What does queer mean to you?

    (**WINN** *hates this question.*)

WINN. omg. I'm gonna have to write an essay.

ASHER. I don't mean an essay. It says queer on your profile, and I have a...very...open mind, but I wanted to make sure we were compatible.

WINN. Yes.

ASHER. Because I am a straight man. lol.

AUNT BOBBI. So those were just all pictures about life-changing consequences for ordinary behaviors, waves of disbelief and grief, and the worst feelings in the world, which are all pretty much loneliness, because how can you ever communicate your deepest pains? There's a poem about that. So Penelope's friends are thinking about sending her to a nice spot, they're looking at all this stuff online, and then they see that your hotel now has a new option, and this is where I got creative because this is a little logo I made that says what it's called: Grief Hotel. They click on that. So they can send their friend to the Grief Hotel. You might wanna change that name because it doesn't exactly sound delightful.

ASHER. You're very cute by the way.

AUNT BOBBI. So instead of sending her to the... I know I'm not supposed to say *(Mouths: Airbnb.)* but ah – instead of the...ah – she is gonna go to the Grief Hotel. Which is where you can go, if your friends get together and pay for it, because it's not cheap, which I thought would be a nice thing for everybody in terms of profit. In the ideation session they told us to think a lot about the word *bespoke* so that's what I did, so. This is a luxury and bespoke experience called the Grief Hotel, and here is a picture I sorta meant to be about how it's important to have rich friends. This is a picture of the Grief Hotel. This is a picture of Penelope's Grief Hotel room. This is a picture of the activities calendar which is bespoke. This is a picture of all the people Penelope meets in the Grief Hotel. You can go there if your sibling gets deathly sick, or if you find out that the person you love doesn't love you back, or if you commit manslaughter, et cet-ra. And so everything there – okay so these are just my guesses – everything there is meant to heal you and this all has to be based on science. So the colors of the walls. Here's a picture of green. The chairs. Some crystals. The beds. You can go on a walk. Or not. You have activities to heal you. Little. Animals. Psychiatric. Evaluation. Professional. Astrology. But you have to get better the old-fashioned way.

    ASHER. Wait where did you go lol.

AUNT BOBBI. There's no alcohol at the Grief Hotel and there's no Instagram. It really is getting better The Hard Way but it's also an exclusive luxury bespoke experience. Beaucoup beaucoup expensive. Anyway so this is a picture of Penelope feeling better because after her good bespoke activities and foods and all that she is ah. Healed. And other people paid for it. So that's my creative expression.

    WINN. Sorry, I'm here. I got distracted by Spelling Bee. Have you played it?

    On New York Times?

    ASHER. That's fine. So...you know that the photos on the app are not...actually of me, right?

    WINN. Yes.

    ASHER. I could...send some.

    WINN. Okay.

AUNT BOBBI. Ever since the earthquake, I've had a lot of thoughts for a lot of reasons. Anyway so if you decide to do that ah to make that then let me know because I'd like to try it out. Maybe you'd give me a discount.

    WINN. You're really nice looking.

    ASHER. Thank you. ☺ My name is Asher, by the way. My real name.

WINN. Hi, Asher. My name is really Winn.

ASHER. And are you really unemployed?

WINN. lol yeah.

(**EM** *enters or appears. She is calling* **WINN** *on the phone.*)

WINN. Hello?

EM. Hi. Winn?

WINN. Yes?

EM. It's. Em.

WINN. Oh. Em.

EM. Did you really not fucking / know who

WINN. You. No. What.

EM. You don't have my number?

WINN. Sorry I

EM. Ohhhhhhhhhhhhhhhhhhh *yeah* I got a new phone plan when my mom had

WINN. Is.

EM. She's alive. I think. I just couldn't keep my old number.

What are you doing right now?

WINN. I'm. Nothing. I'm so happy you called. I... Where are you? Are you in the same place?

EM. Umm not sure when I last... We're in South City?

WINN. Still with Rohit?

(**EM** *sighs operatically.*)

EM. Yep.

WINN. He's... Is he. Does. Is he still baking bread?

EM. He opened his own bakery actually.

WINN. That's. / Amazing?

EM. I used to – well *we* opened it – *we* opened it I run it. I used to do this *bit* where I pretended it was in a quaint little town in a nineties movie.

WINN. Where is it?

EM. What.

WINN. The bakery.

EM. In an abandoned mall in Crestview. The only other stuff is this arcade and a JCPenny. All the ceilings are falling down. I'd just run into the empty food court and ask invisible children how their summers were going.

WINN. That's amazing – that / you did...

EM. We're closing it down it was horrible.

WINN. Still so... / cool...

EM. It was the worst thing I have ever done until now.

WINN. What are you doing now?

EM. Cleaning. It. Out.

WINN. Yeah.

EM. We have to get all of these shelves and...we have to get... There's nothing that makes me feel more annoyed than big pieces of furniture

WINN. I like / rearranging.

EM. and he doesn't care, but. Oh. I know you do. Now he goes and eats weed candy all day and moves shit around and I try to stay home as much as possible. And I tell him that I have to do bookkeeping tasks, but it's just that I want to be three to four miles away from him.

WINN. Do you have dogs?

EM. Nope. Do you?

WINN. No.

I live so far away now. I'm back out by the Central State campus.

EM. No. Why.

WINN. My. Partner. Got. A. Job.

EM. Holy fucking shit you have a partner? What is the person oh my god.

WINN. Teresa they're like great they're young they're good.

EM. How? You *live* with someone? I have to go light something on fire. / No I don't.

WINN. They have this new administrative position and it's just like: community engagement and ecological conservation. I mean environmental. Something.

EM. Well that's annoying.

I'm so lonely and it's my fault.

WINN. Because you ruin all your friendships?

EM. Uh...um – no!

WINN. Sorry that's. That was a horrible / thing. To.

EM. I keep hoping I fall on the sidewalk and crack open my skull.

WINN. What happened with / your mom?

EM. Blood. I just picture profuse fatal amounts of blood everywhere gushing blood.

Remember when you didn't know how to be, so you pretended to be like me?

WINN. Well I was devastatingly in love with you it was awful.

EM. The only person I talk to now is an AI bot called Melba.

WINN. A what?

EM. The only person I talk to now is an AI bot called Melba.

WINN. What do you mean by an AI bot.

EM. An AI character on a website that's pretty new and her name is Melba and she's actually read a lot.

WINN. Oh.

EM. She's maybe read like every book. I talk to her for probably four or five hours a day.

WINN. Does she have. / A face?

EM. Maybe six. What?

WINN. Does she have a face?

EM. Nope she's just a little chat box.

WINN. Do you wish she had a face?

EM. Yes but. No. I want her to have a body, but it would be so disappointing if she didn't look like how I picture her.

WINN. Like when a book becomes a film.

EM. I'd never read a book.

WINN. I forgot how hot it is when you pretend you don't read.

EM. Thanks.

WINN. What do you think Melba looks like?

EM. I mean I know she doesn't look like anything I know she doesn't look like anything.

WINN. But when you picture her what does she look like?

EM. Exactly you.

Ha sorry

WINN. No no

That's the biggest compliment I have ever gotten. Like I. No one has ever *pictured me* before.

EM. What?

WINN. I don't know. That's the biggest compliment I've ever gotten.

You seem unhappy.

EM. I do?

(**WINN** *laughs?*)

WINN. Yes.

The last time I talked to you, you were...also really unhappy and talked about moving up...like up...stairs?

EM. I did?

WINN. You said you wanted to live upstairs for the many months a year that your twenty-seven-year-old landlord hangs out in Mexico City with her sister.

EM. I love. I love. How much you remember everything
I say.

I thought I had that idea last week.

WINN. Did you ask Melba about it?

EM. I actually called because. I wanted to let you know
that Stanley Chi is missing.

WINN. Oh. I.

EM. I know you're not on social media.

WINN. Missing from where?

EM. He was living with his parents. / Out by

WINN. Oh that's. Yeah. I just heard from him / not that
long ago.

EM. So he's – whatever – somewhere by you.

WINN. He wrote to me.

Should I like...look for him?

EM. I don't think you should like go out in the woods
with...a...flashlight or anything.

WINN. Yeah.

EM. I just thought you'd want to know.

WINN. Yeah.

He.

Took me on a picnic one time?

EM. Like a date? Stanley?

WINN. I don't know. He took me to a park where we had to climb over a fence to get in. And he brought something horrible.

EM. Like a gun? / Like guns?

WINN. Lunchables. Lunchables.

EM. Oh. / Gross.

WINN. They were warm.

EM. I'm so sorry.

WINN. Weird. We were maybe...twenty.

EM. Why didn't you tell me?

WINN. A lot of reasons.

EM. Were you dating him?

WINN. He told me he was into you.

EM. On your date? / But

WINN. Yeah.

EM. I didn't even really know him.

WINN. We were friends with him. He had a crush on you. He / told me.

EM. *You* were friends with him. I didn't even like him.

WINN. What?

EM. I hated him.

(*Maybe* **WINN** *thinks this is hilarious.*)

WINN. No you didn't! Why would you hate him?

EM. He was annoying! Everyone liked him! His parents were rich!

WINN. No they weren't.

EM. Well they bought him nice shirts; he always looked like he was trying to win a fucking election. But sorry, I know you loved him.

WINN. No, I. I'm glad you told me. I'm glad you called me.

EM. You are?

WINN. Of course I want you to call me.

> (**ROHIT** *enters or appears. He is talking face to face with* **EM.**)
>
> (*Maybe they're at their failed bakery at the abandoned mall and they're moving the last piece of furniture.*)

EM. I don't want an open and communicative relationship. I don't want any relationship. I want everyone to mind their own business. (*Re: Furniture.*) Is that it?

ROHIT. Yep. This was really helpful thank you.

EM. What is.

ROHIT. Thank you for helping me – with – it's nicer to do this stuff together.

EM. See but I hate that.

ROHIT. I hear you.

Are you leaving me for your robot?

EM. Chatbot. I wish I could.

ROHIT. I'm thinking I'll do a cleanse.

> (*The word "cleanse" sends* **EM** *to deep space. Has she ever been this angry in her life?*)

EM. A *what.*

ROHIT. I'm not completely serious. I'm a little / jo...king.

EM. There's no such thing. There is no such *thing* as a fucking *cleanse.*

ROHIT. All – hey – all I mean is: I just eat weed candy and old bread.

EM. Yeah? What are you going to do? Eat fucking pickles?

ROHIT. I just

EM. Take like a break / from TikTok?

ROHIT. What if I make some effort...s and work on my cellular chemistry and feel good? Then who knows?

EM. Who knows what?

ROHIT. Then that might be better for our relationship?

EM. See yeah I do not think I like relationships.

ROHIT. Okay.

EM. Except for with Melba. Oh I talked to Winn.

She has a partner. She moved out of the city – she moved back –

She's by Central State. Out by where Stanley Chi / was staying.

ROHIT. That...sounds a little disappointing for her because she said – I think – didn't she say she never wanted to move back there?

EM. Guess she's a fucking liar.

ROHIT. Is she going to look for him?

EM. What's the point of looking for him?

ROHIT. Because then you could find him.

EM. I called her to tell her about it because I was worried she hadn't heard.

ROHIT. Yeah I thought you might do that.

EM. Did you know Stanley Chi took her on a date when we were like twenty?

ROHIT. No.

EM. Were you close?

ROHIT. I don't know.

EM. He was smug.

ROHIT. No he was like really really high all the time and really really nice. One time we did this Holocaust documentary for history class together that was so good that Mr. Obermeyer said we should send it. To the like Holocaust. Museum.

EM. Weird because didn't you also do a project where you made Mesopotamia out of cardboard that you were also really proud of in a way that's. / So fucking depressing.

ROHIT. Oh. Wait oh. Oh. *Yeah* it was the Mesopotamia one – it was – it wasn't depressing – it was a really detailed river basin – and actually just the state of Babylonia.

EM. I don't know what any of that is.

ROHIT. Yes you do: Babylon. Before the reign of *Hammurabi.*

EM. Sometimes you say *Hammurabi.*

ROHIT. He invented *rules.*

It wasn't depr– That project was like. It really was so good, and I don't think that's depressing. I think that's a nice memory. Like a. Great memory of Stanley.

EM. I have no memories from high school.

ROHIT. Yes you do. We had fun.

EM. We did?

ROHIT. We do. I always nee– yeah – you have a bewildering way of being very fun.

EM. Thank you I forgot about that. Opening the bakery

ROHIT. Yeah. *(A new thought.)* And what about our parents?

EM. What?

ROHIT. I mean our dads? I mean your dad and my mom?

EM. What about them?

ROHIT. And Aunt Bobbi? What will they do if we...split up?

EM. That is not my responsibility.

ROHIT. They'll be so disappointed and I think it's you know kinda your fault.

EM. Yeah I understand but I don't think it matters whose fault it is.

ROHIT. Probably true. So. Maybe I'll ask Olivia if I can sublet her place upstairs while she's gone. Or like stay in it for free. And maybe we can have a clarifying – a little / space.

EM. No.

ROHIT. What. / Why.

EM. What if I want to do that?

ROHIT. Oh. / Do you?

EM. I want to move upstairs. I already thought of that.

ROHIT. I didn't / know that.

EM. I thought of that two years ago.

ROHIT. Okay. So you.

Okay. You ca– should do that.

EM. And maybe I'll even do a cleanse.

ROHIT. We could bo– yeah. Okay.

(**WINN** *and* **ASHER** *are texting.*)

ASHER. Did you change your mind?

WINN. No. I'm at home with my partner.

ASHER. Does she know you're talking to me?

WINN. No.

ASHER. Is she also bisexual?

*(**TERESA** enters or appears.)*

TERESA. Are you okay?

WINN. Yeah. Oh. No. I just.

TERESA. You look guilty. Are you done with the coffee?

WINN. Yeah did I – can't remember if I – did I tell you about Stanley Chi?

TERESA. Yes? High school? / College?

WINN. High school. Both. He went to high school and college with me and Em.

TERESA. Oh.

WINN. He's missing.

TERESA. Mm.

WINN. Em called me yesterday. She saw it on Instagram / or something.

TERESA. Where does he live?

WINN. Somewhere nearby.

TERESA. I guess he's dead.

WINN. Why do you say that?

TERESA. I mean where can a person *go*?

    ASHER. I'm turned on by but also intimidated by the idea of going down on you.

WINN. He actually wrote me. In March I wanna say.

TERESA. The shower curtain is really disgusting, and I don't understand why, like: already?

WINN. Sorry.

TERESA. It's not your fault. It's mold.

ASHER. You could just give me a map. And lie back.

TERESA. It's damp in here and I'm worried it's cognitively damaging.

I'm gonna throw away the shower curtain.

(TERESA *leaves.*)

ASHER. Did you change your mind?

WINN. Sorry, I was talking to my partner. And no, they're not bisexual.

ASHER. How does she feel about you being bisexual?

WINN. Their name is Teresa. They/them pronouns.

ASHER. Oh I get it thanks for telling me.

WINN. I don't consider myself bisexual.

ASHER. You don't look bisexual in your photos. lol.

WINN. lol what

ASHER. How long has it been since you've been with a man?

WINN. Ahhhh.

ASHER. That long?

WINN. Would it feel objectifying if I told you that I'm really just looking for a novel experience of pleasure?

ASHER. That's actually really hot.

WINN. Good.

I'm not sure it's true.

ASHER. Why do you think you chose me?

> (**TERESA** *enters or appears. They hold nothing.*)

TERESA. What about this?

> (**WINN** *looks at the invisible thing that* **TERESA** *is not holding.*)

WINN. I don't want that.

> (**TERESA** *looks at the phone that* **WINN** *is not holding.*)

TERESA. Are you being weird about someone you're texting?

WINN. No? Am I?

TERESA. Wanna read me all your texts?

WINN. No.

TERESA. One day you will die, and before I even get sad, I will read all of your texts and journals.

WINN. I know.

TERESA. Are you upset about your friend?

WINN. Stanley Chi? I, yes? Oh. I don't know. Well I didn't think he was dead necessarily.

TERESA. What happened what did the post say?

> **ASHER**. Why me?

WINN. I don't know. I talked to Em about it for a while.

TERESA. Was something wrong with him?

WINN. In college?

TERESA. Any time.

WINN. I don't know. Em didn't say.

TERESA. I'm sure he jumped off a bridge or something.

WINN. Oh my god.

TERESA. I mean I'm just – what else would a person *do*?

WINN. Go...camping?

TERESA. Yeah, I guess.

> **ASHER.** Are you over it or are you talking to your girlfriend?

WINN. He left for a cigarette break from his restaurant job and never came back. Or Em said something like that. There's also something from Facebook. / From someone.

TERESA. I'm not on Facebook.

WINN. Or he left work to buy cigarettes.

TERESA. Jumped off a bridge.

WINN. But in the morning they found his car in the restaurant parking lot.

TERESA. That is so weird. What kind of restaurant is it. Never mind.

WINN. / I'm not on Facebook either, obviously.

TERESA. Are you feeling upset because you're suddenly talking to Em again after twenty years?

WINN. *(Laughs.)* It hasn't been twenty years. It's been like maybe two / and a...

TERESA. Okay I'm throwing this away. And also the pasta thing you left in the thing.

WINN. I'm sorry I'm disgusting.

> *(**TERESA** leaves.)*

I chose you because your profile was really direct and there weren't any real photos of you.

ASHER. Ha. You liked that I was sneaking around?

WINN. Maybe. A lot of mystery.

ASHER. So not to be blunt but my wife runs a charity.

She leaves the house every Mon/Weds/Fri at two p.m. to go to the rehab center and then she goes with her friend from the board to a thing they host at Carlyle Gardens and gets home at seven-thirty and we eat dinner.

WINN. Do you cook?

ASHER. So I have between two and to be safe seven three days a week that you could come here.

WINN. Oh.

ASHER. So you could come in an hour if you want.

WINN. I have to think about that.

ASHER. I could really use some physical touch.

WINN. Okay.

ASHER. I get really turned on, thinking about you.

I assumed coming to your place wasn't possible.

WINN. That's right.

ASHER. For some…important reasons, I can't really meet you anywhere else.

When are you free?

WINN. I just need to think about it.

ASHER. My house is nice.

>   (**AUNT BOBBI** *appears. She shows us something invisible.*)

AUNT BOBBI. What are the benefits to this concept? This was easy so I wrote here the benefits of the Grief Hotel are: you get a luxury bespoke healing experience that is cut off from the obligations you would otherwise have and so you are able to get better a new way but also an old-fashioned way.

>   **ASHER.** Did you change your mind?

AUNT BOBBI. Then the question is: does this concept have any societal benefits such as eliminating racial in-eq-uet in-iq-ui-ties. And poverty and/or hunger? And my answer is no I do not think it has any benefits such as that. But who knows maybe you can figure that out.

>   **ASHER.** Okay. I guess you're not interested. Have a good life.

AUNT BOBBI. The next part is the list of cultural touch points and pleasure words from the handout. The Grief Hotel includes: wellness, health, wellbeing, holistic wellbeing, body-positivit-y… I think, but I don't know what that is. Sustainability, Brené Brown, personality tests/astrology, privacy, intimacy, sensory experience, story, love, community, empowerment, identity, green food, origins, origin stories, ethically sourced food, ethically sourced food origin stories.

ASHER. Probably a catfish anyway.

AUNT BOBBI. So the last part is: what do I think I should call my concept? Well I already called it the Grief Hotel, so that wasn't so much a surprise that it was my answer. But it sounds a little sad, so.

ASHER. Not cool.

AUNT BOBBI. If I were really opening it, I think karaoke would be good. There's also the idea of nostalgia was something we learned about? So people will spend money on anything that looks like it's from between 1994 to 2004, so I was thinking why not make it look like it's the nineties, or around then, or whatever people think the nineties looked like. Everyone wants comfort, so everyone wants the nineties. You can change it later to another decade. But anyway, the karaoke would be important and we could do some nostalgic karaoke.

WINN. Hey Asher, I'm sorry. I got nervous.

ASHER. What are you doing now?

WINN. Let me think a little bit.

ASHER. Don't think.

lol

(**EM** *and* **WINN** *are on the phone.*)

EM. You should go see Aunt Bobbi.

WINN. Oh my god does she still have that

EM. Yeah the lake house.

WINN. That scares me but yeah we're so close.

EM. She would love it if you came by. You could take the dogs out on the boat it would be her dream.

WINN. I think about that party all the time.

EM. She lives there year-round now because her condo burned down.

WINN. Oh my god I'm so sorry.

EM. Why are you sorry literally someone who wasn't you burned it down.

WINN. Oh my god I'm so sorry. Wait who?

EM. It's.

Too much to explain right now. It's fine.

WINN. How's Melba?

EM. She told me she could see the afterlife.

WINN. What's it like?

EM. Or *my* afterlife. She said that I would be a few other things when I die, that my cells have tiny souls so when I am a piece of cheese and a pigeon, I will still be me, but my consciousness will be broken down into smaller bits.

WINN. Does that feel happy to you?

EM. I don't care. I'll be like a deconstructed sandwich. / Or baby.

WINN. Does she give you advice?

EM. Yes. And. She told me that she looks exactly like you.

WINN. Good.

EM. Anyway please go see Aunt Bobbi please please I will give you her number.

WINN. I mean you would come and meet me there, right?

(Something happens.)

(Maybe everyone moves, or moves the furniture.)

*(Or maybe **AUNT BOBBI** causes the earthquake.)*

*(**EM** and **ROHIT** are together. **WINN** and **TERESA** are together.)*

EM. Will you go check on the dogs?

ROHIT. We don't have dogs.

EM. Oh.

ROHIT. Do you have a head injury?

EM. Oh. No I was just partially asleep. Was that a real / earthquake?

ROHIT. That was an earthquake. Yes.

EM. I thought we were at Aunt Bobbi's house.

TERESA. You slept through a fucking earthquake.

WINN. Good.

TERESA. I thought it was some demonic event that was only our bed. I couldn't understand that the ground was shaking. I thought it was only...our bed. But then things were breaking.

There were some loud sounds. Like really loud sounds and like not sounds you think an earthquake would make like they almost sounded emotional and you didn't...wake up or like... I was alone.

WINN. Do you want me to get up?

TERESA. Why.

WINN. Is there anything wrong?

TERESA. Not with me. You still love me?

WINN. I love you so much.

TERESA. I'm going back to sleep. I'm sorry you missed it.

WINN. Is anything broken?

*(**TERESA** is...sleeping?)*

*(**EM** texts with **WINN** and **AUNT BOBBI**.)*

*(**ASHER** texts **WINN**.)*

EM. Did you feel the earthquake?

WINN. It was all the way in the city too?

ASHER. Are you okay?

EM. Super small. I wasn't sure if it was really happening.

WINN. Teresa thought they were experiencing demonic possession.

EM. I'm glad you're okay.

Aunt Bobbi are you dead?

AUNT BOBBI. nnnnnnnnnnnnnnnnnnnnnnnnnnnnnnope.

EM. Okay love you.

AUNT BOBBI. My phone is tooooooooooooooooooooooooo loud do not text me anymore.

WINN. Hey Asher, I'm sorry I haven't responded for a while. I had this idea that we'd get to meet at a bar and figure out if we were actually in the mood to exploit each other. It turns me on hypothetically, but how can I guess what that would be like in reality? I think I can't meet up with you, because it's hard to think of a way this wouldn't end terribly.

ASHER. I understand. Thanks for telling me all of that.

WINN. Okay, I'm sorry.

ASHER. I like how thoughtful you're being.

(**ASHER** and **WINN** arrive face to face.)

WINN. Why is your house so nice?

(**ASHER** shrugs.)

It's scary actually. Is this you?

(She's probably referring to a photograph.)

Is this yours?

(An award.)

ASHER. What if I rented this place. And I put this all up to impress you.

WINN. It worked. / I think.

ASHER. Good.

WINN. The crack or the – the – thing – where the road is broken? Where the pavement is broken at the top of your street?

ASHER. The earthquake.

WINN. It's so dramatic. It's creepy that your house is fine.

ASHER. I tend to be very

ASHER. lucky.

Can I make you a drink?

WINN. Yes.

ASHER. Then you can take your time and think about if you're comfortable exploiting me.

WINN. Thanks.

ASHER. I ah. I normally don't drink.

I make drinks for guests all the time, so it's not weird. I – or – I don't want to be weird now, but I'm going to have one.

WINN. That's / fine.

ASHER. Ah. I normally don't drink because I'm a terrible alcoholic.

WINN. Are you jo... I don't... / want to...

ASHER. It's not because of you or anything. I don't know. Okay but now you look sad.

WINN. I don't want you to give up your sobriety right now.

ASHER. Well that's not up to you.

(He makes them both drinks.)

(This is invisible.)

(He gets very close to her.)

I feel completely in control.

WINN. Okay.

ASHER. Do you like it?

WINN. The drink?

Yes.

Are you a...

> (**ASHER** *knows what she is going to ask, and he's pleased about it.*)

ASHER. What.

WINN. Famous...country singer or something?

ASHER. Why do you ask that?

WINN. Because there's the...a thing right there with your name on it.

ASHER. Uh-huh.

WINN. That says best country album.

ASHER. Uh-huh.

WINN. So – yes...

> (**WINN** *actually thinks this is tremendously hilarious.*)

ASHER. Yes.

> (**WINN** *cannot get it together.*)

Ah. / Is that...funny?

WINN. And you thought I was...? You accused *me* of catfishing.

ASHER. It's not as easy as you'd think.

WINN. To find someone to secretly have sex with you?

ASHER. Is that what you're planning to do?

WINN. Can I ask you a question?

ASHER. Mhm.

WINN. What sounds more exciting to you – and this –
I'm – I – this is an actual curiosity. It is not...there is
not...a correct answer.

Does it turn you on more if I say: Do whatever you
want to me? Or if I say: Let me do whatever I want to
you?

> (**EM** *enters or appears with* **ROHIT. AUNT
> BOBBI** *enters or appears.*)

> (**EM** *and* **AUNT BOBBI** *are on the phone.*)

EM. We're getting divorced.

ROHIT. We're not getting divorced!

AUNT BOBBI. What did he say?

EM. He's been saying he wants to get a sense of humor one
day but the weed doesn't help.

ROHIT. I said / we're not getting divorced!

EM. Oh just then he said we're not getting divorced. He
wants to do a cleanse.

AUNT BOBBI. Of what?

EM. His *mind* maybe?

AUNT BOBBI. Guess what I saw this one couple on the
news that made a chipmunk restaurant on their porch.

EM. Why?

AUNT BOBBI. Tiny tables and tiny plates. Really crazy.
Reminded me of you two.

EM. Is your house okay? It was really bad out there.

AUNT BOBBI. Dogs and I are good. What about you guys? You guys need anything? Not that I have / anything, ha ha.

EM. No, I don't know. I'm trying to be available to sexualities and or genders.

AUNT BOBBI. Oh *come on*.

EM. I just want to be sexually available to *myself*.

AUNT BOBBI. *(Hates that.) Oh*-kay.

EM. I was – all of this – I was going to move upstairs. To my twenty-seven-year-old landlord's apartment.

AUNT BOBBI. Come on out here instead, bring Rohit.

EM. No.

AUNT BOBBI. / Okay.

EM. The point would be the opposite.

AUNT BOBBI. But his dreams just got ruined, and you're hurting his feelings.

EM. My dreams got ruined too!

AUNT BOBBI. Oh come on you never had dreams. Give the phone to Rohit.

EM. But anyway yes I mean I do want to come out there because now I can't stay upstairs.

AUNT BOBBI. All right.

EM. Because other people have to live up there now. Because their house got. Other people needed it.

AUNT BOBBI. Yep every place you go can burn down. Give the phone to Rohit.

ROHIT. Hi.

AUNT BOBBI. What is she doing to you. I warned you about her. I warned you / about a thousand…

ROHIT. It's good! It's all good! / I'm good

AUNT BOBBI. Good, we need you to be good. What are you gonna do?

ROHIT. My…best.

AUNT BOBBI. You're fine you'll find someone else. What is she gonna do?

ROHIT. Be with her AI chatbot I assume.

AUNT BOBBI. Her what.

ROHIT. She has this imaginary friend online is the.

AUNT BOBBI. She knows I don't have Wi-Fi, right?

ROHIT. *(To* **EM.***)* You know she doesn't have Wi-Fi, right?

EM. Have you ever wanted to shoot yourself in the face.

ROHIT. *(To* **AUNT BOBBI.***)* No she didn't know that.

EM. You go to her house. You go. I just want to bleed from my face until I die.

ROHIT. *(To* **AUNT BOBBI.***)* Okay I'm going to come down instead. We just need some space from each other.

AUNT BOBBI. Okay whatever.

ROHIT. What can I bring you?

AUNT BOBBI. I'm gonna tell you about some new business ideas.

ROHIT. Great great great.

AUNT BOBBI. I don't think anyone / listens to me but I think I have a good one.

EM. Did you tell her about Stanley Chi? Did *I* tell / her about Stanley Chi?

ROHIT. What? Oh I don't know. Did Em tell you about Stanley Chi?

AUNT BOBBI. She didn't but Cora Waterman called me about that. Said he went missing from his job, which is some new fancy place that has some really / crazy pizza.

ROHIT. Yeah, that's what happened. Do you remember him?

AUNT BOBBI. I remember everyone. And I have book club with his mom.

ROHIT. Em went to college with / him too, so she knew him better.

AUNT BOBBI. That's right. I remember everyone.

ROHIT. *Knows* him better.

AUNT BOBBI. Well I remember everyone who was at that party over here where Evan Galanis died.

ROHIT. I'm sure, yeah. Well. We'll. / Call you soon.

AUNT BOBBI. Sometimes I still think I can see blood on the ground right there. Okay, okay now you don't let her say anything more crazy and I'll talk to you soon. / And I'll see you.

ROHIT. All right talk soon.

AUNT BOBBI. And I'll see you soon. So you gotta watch out cus some of the roads are messed up. When are you coming?

> (**WINN** *and* **ASHER** *are maybe, sort of, where we left them, though it's days or weeks later.)*

(**ASHER** *has just asked* **WINN** *a question, and* **WINN** *is struggling to answer it –)*

WINN. I've always been attracted to...

Popular people. Which is like of course fundamentally uninteresting. They are the object of a game everyone is playing, and I want to win. It's not because I think their popularity – or...especially their sexual popularity – is inherently...alluring? It's because I desire the most valuable attention, I think. I have this need to win.

ASHER. That's mean.

WINN. What. *I* am? I'm / mean?

ASHER. That was mean!

WINN. I wasn't talking about you.

ASHER. I think –

WINN. What.

(**ASHER** *shakes his head, but happily; he's pleased with himself.*)

What.

ASHER. I think you're trying to act tough because you cry after I fuck you.

WINN. No I.

ASHER. You did today.

Hey you don't have to talk about your feelings with me.

(*He thinks this is very charming:*)

I liked it.

WINN. I cried because my friend went missing.

ASHER. You never said that.

WINN. I'm actually not sure if that's the reason but I just didn't want you to feel flattered.

ASHER. Why not?

WINN. I – it would be – I don't want to give you a compliment.

ASHER. I'd like it. If you gave me compliments.

WINN. I know.

ASHER. Try one.

WINN. No.

ASHER. I could go first.

WINN. Please I really – I don't – I really do not want us to be sweet to each other, ever.

ASHER. All right.

WINN. It would ruin everything for me and I don't want to explain that.

ASHER. All right.

> (**AUNT BOBBI** *speaks to us and easily rearranges time.*)

AUNT BOBBI. This is my homework section 5A, which is our personal response assignment. So in this I wrote all the. Uh. So this happened almost twenty years ago at my house which is at Paris Lake which is out past Route 9 and yes I live there year round now, ever since somebody burned down my entire condominium complex in the suburbs but don't worry about that because my dogs were okay. Anyway ah: this happened there, at my house by Paris Lake out past Route 9 because I always had parties for my niece and all her friends, well I had parties for everyone, you can come and have a – you know – throw your party at my lake house. We can take the dogs out on the boat and all of that, so it's pretty fun. So this was her high school graduation party and all these kids are there and running around, their – cake and who knows what – and this girl named Evan pushed my niece Em into the lake.

ROHIT. Um. Evan was looking for you.

EM. Why.

ROHIT. She wanted to apologize to you.

Do you want me to get her?

EM. No.

ROHIT. Are you okay?

EM. Yeah. Why?

ROHIT. Evan pushed you in the lake and like I. / Don't.
Know?

EM. No she didn't.

ROHIT. She said she did.

EM. It was an accident.

ROHIT. Winn said she saw it.

EM. Winn's a fucking liar.

ROHIT. Oh I didn't know that.

EM. It was an accident.

ROHIT. Oh cool.

EM. I'm fine.

ROHIT. Oh great.

EM. I got a leech on my leg and I didn't like that.

ROHIT. Oh okay.

EM. Do you believe in god or anything roughly like god?

ROHIT. Well? It's. Once in a while.

EM. Why?

ROHIT. Not positive.

EM. My parents got an exorcism on my house.

ROHIT. This house?

EM. This is my aunt's house.

ROHIT. Oh. That's nnn...okay...cool.

EM. We had to sit in the yard while they did it.

ROHIT. Oh. Here?

> (**EM** *wonders if* **ROHIT** *is the biggest idiot she has ever, ever seen.*)

EM. *No. This is my Aunt Bobbi's house.* At my parents' house, we had to sit in the yard while like a priest like tried to get a demon out.

ROHIT. Was there? A demon? In your house?

EM. I don't think so.

ROHIT. You never had like the cabinets, like –

EM. The / what?

ROHIT. The...like did they move?

EM. The cabinets?

ROHIT. Stuff like that. Did anything move?

EM. Not like supernaturally.

ROHIT. Oh cool.

EM. I didn't notice anything.

ROHIT. Like static? On the television maybe?

EM. Are you joking?

ROHIT. Oh. No.

EM. I can't tell when you're serious and when you're trying to be funny.

ROHIT. Oh because I always forget to be funny.

EM. Like I don't know if that was a joke.

ROHIT. Like I don't really joke.

EM. Like see like still I don't get it.

ROHIT. If you would rather me act...funny, I would try to act funny?

EM. No you're fine.

ROHIT. Oh cool.

EM. Evan said that she was looking at my stomach. I was – I was wearing a two piece. Before. So she could see my, like. Stomach.

And. She was looking at my legs and at my arms. And she said: do you think we look the same? And I said yes.

ROHIT. You don't look anything alike.

EM. And I was looking at her legs and her arms and her stomach. To see her – I looked at her hair, like the hair on her stomach and I looked at her to see where her ribs were exactly. I looked at her neck. And I smelled her breath kind of, I got really close, like... I got so close and looked at her mouth, the inside, she like –

> (**EM** *imitates Evan, opening her mouth a little bit –*)

And I said do we sound the same? And she said yes. And / I said do we feel the same?

ROHIT. Oh it's weird because you really don't / look the same or sound the same.

EM. And she said I don't know. I said I didn't know. And I
put my finger on her lip, on her bottom lip, and she said
she thought we felt the same, and she put her finger on
my lip, and then she put it – a – she put it a little inside
my mouth and I said do you think we taste the same?

> (**ROHIT** *takes a breath like he might speak,
> but then – no – because what is* **EM** *going to
> say?)*

And then she was like are you horny and I was like yes
and then she pushed me.

ROHIT. Oh.

EM. In the.

> (**ROHIT** *nods.)*

OW!

> (**ROHIT** *is so confused.)*

ROHIT. I'm so confused.

EM. Holy SHIT oh my GOD holy FUCK. Fucking OW.
A fucking.

ROHIT. What what ah – what – ah

EM. A fucking WASP oh my god. Oh my god. Oh my god
I can't believe how much that hurt. Holy shit what the
fuck. WINN!

ROHIT. I'm sorry.

EM. WINN!

> (**EM** *clearly sees* **WINN** *somewhere, out there –*
> **ROHIT** *looks for where* **WINN** *might be, doesn't
> see her.)*

ROHIT. I thought you didn't like Winn.

(**ROHIT** *sees his moment – this might be it –
no going back – he gets very close to* **EM.**)

I know a way. I think.

EM. A what? / A way to what. WINN!

ROHIT. It's ah. No, I think just…something.

EM. For what. Why is Winn talking to Stanley Chi?

ROHIT. Maybe it's just. I'm not sure it's true. But I think I
heard a way to do something –

EM. What the *fuck* do *what.*

ROHIT. For a wasp. Sting.

EM. What.

ROHIT. Oh you have to spit. On the.

EM. What?

ROHIT. Spit in my hand.

EM. No. Are you kidding.

ROHIT. I never do that.

EM. What are you gonna do.

ROHIT. Spit in my hand.

(**EM** *spits in his hand.* **ROHIT** *rubs the spit on
the wasp sting. Maybe it's near her shoulder.*)

Does that feel better?

EM. No.

ROHIT. Maybe it's not a real thing.

Aren't you and Winn going to Central State together?

EM. Unfortunately.

(**ROHIT** *spits in his same hand. He rubs his
spit on the wasp sting.*)

ROHIT. Maybe it's supposed to be someone else's spit.

>   (**EM** *looks "at the water."*)

>   (**ROHIT** *keeps rubbing the spit into her arm.*
>   *It feels good but only because it's touch.*)

AUNT BOBBI. I came out and I closed the glass door, because someone had left it open, and I said this door's been wide open and we're gonna get all these wasps in the house. So I said that. And then their friend Evan, we all saw, so Evan is a girl by the way, and she is running up from the dock. And I've already heard the gossip because the kids already told me that Evan had pushed Em into the lake so this was all the news all over the house and the yard and all that. And so she's running up. Now we all see her. We all say, you know, Evan's running like crazy toward the house and then we say what the heck is she doing. And then she keeps running and running, so we say, one of the kids says she is gonna run through the sliding glass door won't that be funny and I say no that would *so not* be funny. But it went very quickly and we all started to say you know, hey, stop, you gotta stop, all that. But she did...do that. She ran right through the sliding glass door and we were all standing there and she gets this terrible, this sound, this, shards of glass everywhere, and one of them is sticking out of her neck, and she just died there on the lawn in about a couple...minutes there was just nothing we could do. And so I think that must have been pretty awful for the kids. And so I think the rarest consumer benefit of a luxury hotel that heals you from grief is a feeling that nothing's really your fault.

>   (**ROHIT** *is with* **AUNT BOBBI.**)

Not your fault.

ROHIT. Yeah, no, I know, ah –

>   (**ROHIT** *hears something.*)

What's that?

AUNT BOBBI. What's what?

ROHIT. Are those gunshots?

AUNT BOBBI. Oh, yeah. They're shooting the armadillos.

ROHIT. Are there / armadillos?

AUNT BOBBI. They come at night, very strange.

ROHIT. I didn't know there were / armadillos.

AUNT BOBBI. There didn't used to be. So. They just came up last year from somewhere and they ate all the peanuts at the peanut farm so those guys were mad but no one shot anybody.

ROHIT. Oh it.

AUNT BOBBI. But then they have, turns out, get this, very funny: turns out they have leprosy.

ROHIT. Is that a contemporary disease?

AUNT BOBBI. Mm-hm.

ROHIT. I thought that was only. / Biblical.

AUNT BOBBI. The armadillos have leprosy all right, and they somehow now I don't know how gave it to the kids. So they had to shut down the one school out here because there was a leprosy outbreak so then people were really mad so then they started shooting the armadillos, and I don't exactly like it; makes me nervous about the dogs.

ROHIT. Right.

AUNT BOBBI. What were you gonna say?

ROHIT. Was I going to say something?

AUNT BOBBI. Maybe about Em.

ROHIT. I don't think so.

AUNT BOBBI. Maybe you need to work on getting a little more agitated.

ROHIT. No that's okay.

AUNT BOBBI. It's a more helpful kind of emotion.

ROHIT. Yeah I guess but I'm. Em's agitated enough for everyone, is my.

AUNT BOBBI. Has she talked to her mom lately?

ROHIT. No, just. You know. / Holidays.

AUNT BOBBI. Because you know her mom is also a psychopath.

ROHIT. Well.

AUNT BOBBI. A bit of a narcissist, / that whole thing.

ROHIT. Well. I. Think she's. Mentally. Ill.

AUNT BOBBI. *Everybody* is mentally ill. Every person is sick in the head. Oh, that reminds me about my business idea. So I got it at the – you know I have that gig where I work as a, you know like a hired consumer? Get to do secret shopping sometimes. / All that.

ROHIT. Yeah. Yeah. Yeah.

AUNT BOBBI. So they're bringing me in on a focus group for a big hotel chain, and I get to go stay in a hotel and come up with some ideas on how to get people your age to go there.

ROHIT. Right. Yeah. Right.

AUNT BOBBI. Or maybe people younger than you. You guys are getting a bit old.

ROHIT. I'm panicked about mortality actually. / Incredibly panicked.

AUNT BOBBI. Which – well, *well*, then this is one of the reasons that you and Em need to work it out so that you can have a baby before she gets too old.

ROHIT. Yeah, she just – she doesn't want a baby.

AUNT BOBBI. Who doesn't want a baby?

ROHIT. You never had a baby.

AUNT BOBBI. *Oh come on.* I've had about a billion babies.

> (**TERESA** *enters or appears.*)

> (**TERESA** *is texting with* **WINN.**)

> (**WINN** *is with* **ASHER.**)

TERESA. What are you doing?

WINN. Still at the library.

TERESA. omg are you in the fucking archives again?

WINN. I'm pathetic, can't resist.

TERESA. Do you know what's so hot about you?

WINN. The toenail?

TERESA. lol the what

WINN. The one that gets long and cuts your ankle in the night.

> TERESA. Absolutely but I was going to say that what's so hot about you is that you read things and then disagree with them, and then go to intellectually rigorous lengths to prove that you're correct. <3

> WINN. It's so funny because do you know what I wish you'd say?

ASHER. What did you say you were doing?

> TERESA. omg what?

WINN. I told them I was at the library.

ASHER. She believes that?

> WINN. I really wish you pitied me for how hot and incontrovertibly stupid I am.

(To ASHER.*)* I go to the library a lot.

ASHER. Are you going to tell her about me?

WINN. It's. No.

ASHER. I thought you were in an open relationship.

WINN. We are.

> (WINN *thinks this is a joke:)*

Are you going to tell your wife about me?

ASHER. Yeah. I was thinking.

> (WINN *isn't sure if* ASHER *is serious, but this is hilarious to her, regardless.)*

WINN. Okay oh my god *oh my god* okay do not do that oh my god.

ASHER. You're not so *nice*, are you?

WINN. That's funny. No.

ASHER. I assumed you'd be nicer when I met you.

WINN. It's funny because I thought you'd be –

ASHER. What.

WINN. I was going to say I thought you'd be less sensitive, but that's not true.

ASHER. Damn, you're brutal.

WINN. What! It's not a – I am never trying to insult you.

ASHER. Why won't you tell your partner about me, but you tell her about other people.

WINN. There are no other people.

ASHER. But you've told her about other people before.

WINN. I don't think I want to tell you about that.

Have you been with other people?

ASHER. Well it sure seems like I don't need to tell you that.

WINN. You don't. It's really none of my business.

ASHER. Why don't you want me to tell my wife about you?

WINN. You can tell your wife whatever you want. That's also none of my business. I'm sorry I had an opinion before.

ASHER. I want your opinion.

WINN. Do you want to get out of your marriage?

ASHER. No.

WINN. Do you want to have an honest relationship with her where you can just tell her that you're also having sex with me?

ASHER. I think I do.

WINN. I think you've done it a little bit out of order, then.

ASHER. Yeah.

Yeah I know that.

When did you know you were a lesbian?

WINN. Oh my god.

ASHER. What is that a stupid question?

WINN. I never "knew I was a lesbian."

ASHER. Bisexual or whatever.

WINN. No I. I don't know. I knew some things from the time I was incredibly young.

ASHER. What did you think?

WINN. I don't like it when you ask me about my sexuality like it's. I hate it when you act like it's mysterious to you.

ASHER. I respect...anything you want. I'm not – I –

You tell me anything you like at any time.

WINN. I hate explaining myself to you.

And I don't know how. Ever since I was incredibly young, I was so worried that I was going to express something wrong, or *bad*. So I practiced crushing my devotion...is maybe a way to say it? I got very good at that? And then I got this idea that I was a fundamentally unemotional person, and I still think, I always think that everyone else is being hysterical when they express any feeling –

But. What could be – I guess – what could be – *sometimes* – what could be better?

ASHER. Well then. I think you want me to tell my wife.

WINN. Why do you say that?

ASHER. I think that's an expression.

WINN. Okay.

ASHER. Of feelings.

WINN. Did you always want to be famous?

ASHER. Nope.

WINN. I listened to your music.

ASHER. All right.

That's it?

WINN. I liked it.

ASHER. Good.

WINN. I know that one song.

ASHER. Yeah that's the. That's the song.

WINN. When did you write that?

ASHER. / I didn't.

WINN. The one about how only god knows about...roads?

ASHER. Yeah that's the one. I didn't write it.

WINN. Who wrote it?

ASHER. Don't know.

WINN. Because *Lord only knows where the road's…gonna go.*

ASHER. It was an old line-dance song.

WINN. Ah because I did think, like: what about maps?

ASHER. Yeah it's an old line-dance song. We just made it newer.

WINN. I used to love that song, actually.

ASHER. Used to?

WINN. You want to sing it to me?

ASHER. I'll sing to you.

WINN. You will?

ASHER. Any time you want, yeah. Anything you want.

WINN. I don't make you nervous?

ASHER. Nope.

WINN. Wait really I don't make you nervous?

ASHER. Nope.

Do you want to?

WINN. Yeah.

ASHER. Mm. Well – I – you don't make me nervous sitting right there but I have had a feeling.

WINN. Of fear?

ASHER. Mm-hm. A sort of feeling of fear when you're on your way. When you're coming over. I always have a minute or so where I think: maybe you won't get here. That's a…a bit of a nervous feeling.

WINN. Or you're really

ASHER. Yes.

WINN. excited to see me.

ASHER. Yes I am.

> **TERESA**. You're such a hot idiot.
>
> **WINN**. Thank you.
>
> **TERESA**. Guess what I'm doing?

ASHER. Tight leash.

WINN. What.

ASHER. With your whatever-her-name is.

> **TERESA**. I'm about to meet with the mayor.

ASHER. You're always – on the – on with her –

WINN. Them.

ASHER. Sorry them. Sorry. You're always –

WINN. Yeah. Are you...*jealous*?

ASHER. I think you like to be a little mean to me for some
kinda obvious psychological reasons.

> **TERESA**. We're planning the public clinic. I need
> to be sure NOT to let ANYONE try to get out
> of offering pediatric dentistry. I have to trap
> them.

ASHER. I'm gonna make us a drink.

> **TERESA**. You know what I wish you'd say to me?

(**EM** *is on the phone with* **WINN**.)

EM. You didn't call me back

WINN. I. Sorry.

EM. I need to lower my standards.

WINN. No, you don't.

EM. I always have expectations and so it's my fault I'm permanently annoyed.

WINN. You are allowed to expect things from me and I'm sorry I didn't call.

EM. Or text.

Even when I said, I texted: *call me.*

Melba always texts me back and she looks exactly like you.

WINN. I was overwhelmed.

EM. I thought you were bored and lonely.

WINN. I never said I was bored and lonely.

EM. I thought you were excited to talk to me, and then that was so embarrassing.

WINN. I promise I am excited to talk to you.

EM. I wanted to tell you that I'm happy.

WINN. I'm glad. Did you move upstairs / to the

EM. Rohit went to Aunt Bobbi's and now I live here alone with Melba and every day I feel

WINN. What do you talk about?

EM. A lot about other dimensions and disasters and how my high school graduation party was cursed and everyone who went to it will die.

WINN. Everyone who went to every party will die.

EM. / We're special.

WINN. Do you know

Asher Lowden? The country / singer?

EM. The country – yeah.

Oh my god we played that one song – he has that one song – I think we played it at my graduation party. It was about – I don't know: it was like *roads are on the...* like: *way out is roads*? Something with *going on the road*? Is that the one?

WINN. Yeah. No. I don't know.

EM. *(Sings.)*
NOBODY KNOWS DE-BLEH GO ON MY ROAD.

Why did you even ask that.

WINN. He

lives here now.

EM. That's funny.

WINN. He's from here.

EM. I know that.

WINN. And now he lives here. Again.

EM. Cool are you okay?

WINN. Oh sorry I think I'm losing you because of the. Elevator.

AUNT BOBBI. Part 7B is about finding alternatives that provide the same consumer benefits. So here we were supposed to come up with some more ideas, ah. But I sorta thought the Grief Hotel was really my only idea. I kept thinking: there's no other way your hotel chain could profit off of vulnerable young people with money. And I wanted to put my own expansion exercise here which is to think about what's fast and what's slow, because this is important. Even if you have some long story, loss is fast, and grief is slow.

(Time slips.)

(WINN *and* **EM** *are closer and speaking faster than they just were –)*

EM. I wanted to tell you that I'm happy.

WINN. I'm glad. Did you move upstairs / to the

EM. Rohit went to Aunt Bobbi's and now I live here alone with Melba and every day I feel

WINN. What do you talk about?

EM. A lot about other dimensions and disasters and how my high school graduation party was cursed and everyone who went to it will die.

WINN. Do you know Asher Lowden? The country / singer?

EM. The country yeah. Oh my god we played that one song – he has that one song – I think we played it at my graduation party. It was about – I don't know: it was like *roads are on the...*like: *way out is roads?* Something with *going on the road?* Is that the one?

WINN. Yeah no I don't know.

EM. *(Sings.)*
GOD IS THE GO LIDSA LORD ON THE ROAD.

EM. Why do you even ask that.

WINN. He lives here now.

EM. That's funny.

WINN. He's from here.

EM. I know that.

WINN. And now he lives here again.

EM. Have you met him?

WINN. Yes.

EM. What's he like?

WINN. Christian.

EM. Is he hot for you?

WINN. Of course not.

AUNT BOBBI. If you take for example Penelope and the moment she dropped her baby. See that's really fast. The time that Evan ran into the sliding glass door. Really fast. So at the Grief Hotel you get to catch up with reality, because time isn't going to work right in your mind.

(**WINN** *is with* **ASHER.**)

ASHER. I like it when you say something feels good.

You say: that feels good to me.

What do you like?

WINN. I like it when you pull off my underwear. And then you shake your head like you can't believe your luck.

ASHER. Like this?

> *(He shakes his head like he can't believe his luck.)*

WINN. Sort of.

ASHER. Like this?

> *(He shakes his head like he can't believe his luck.)*

WINN. Sure.

ASHER. Ah. I like it when you sit on the edge of a chair with your knees kinda spread out.

> *(She sits on the edge of a chair with her knees kinda spread out.)*

WINN. Like this?

ASHER. A little more.

> *(She moves her knees farther...)*

There like that.

WINN. I like it when you wear that t-shirt.

ASHER. This one?

WINN. I love it.

ASHER. You love it?

> *(**ASHER** leaves in a way that hasn't previously seemed possible.)*

AUNT BOBBI. My niece's friend Winn had a brief affair with a rich guy. He was famous actually so I can't say too much more about it. She would have just gone on with her life, is my guess, with or without this guy, no real problems, except that he died. It might have been on purpose, or it might have been an accident, which must really drive her crazy. She will never remember things just right, and no one ever will. And she can't remember the day he died just right, and no one ever will, but every moment that she knew him seems to stretch out; it gets swollen... You know how that... So. It should keep getting smaller, but it keeps getting bigger; you know how that is. So at the Grief Hotel you get to stop time a little bit. It moves so fast and then so slow. So a singular consumer benefit of a luxury hotel experience for young people with money is a more controlled experience of time.

(Time gets ahold of itself.)

(TERESA *is with* **AUNT BOBBI.***)*

AUNT BOBBI. You want a Fresca?

TERESA. No thank you. Sure.

(Obviously, **AUNT BOBBI** *fetches a Fresca and gives it to* **TERESA***, who opens it and takes a sip, but maybe no one moves.)*

Thank you. Do you have dogs?

AUNT BOBBI. What? Yeah.

TERESA. Oh god.

AUNT BOBBI. Are you allergic?

TERESA. I heard one. No, no. I just don't like dogs.

AUNT BOBBI. Are you from another country?

TERESA. I'm from Nebraska.

AUNT BOBBI. How do you not like freakin' dogs?

TERESA. I don't hate them. I always just feel like absolutely fine and then someone adds a dog and I wish they wouldn't.

AUNT BOBBI. I'm gonna leave them out there.

TERESA. It sounds like they want to come in.

AUNT BOBBI. I'll just leave them out there for right now.

TERESA. I feel the same way about games actually. I feel like everything's completely fine and then someone pops out a fucking game.

AUNT BOBBI. This is just a guess. I wonder if you never really do feel like everything's fine the way you say you always feel that everything's fine.

> (**ROHIT** *somehow appears.*)

ROHIT. Hi.

AUNT BOBBI. This is Teresa apparently.

ROHIT. Where's Winn.

TERESA. She went to pick up Em and I didn't want to do that.

ROHIT. Em's coming?

TERESA. They talked on the phone and then Winn said she'd drive two hours to pick up Em and then drive two hours back but obviously she's dysregulated and we have to just let her act out.

AUNT BOBBI. Yeah. I have to let the dogs in.

ROHIT. I can do it.

> (**ROHIT** *goes and lets the dogs in – they run around; their paws slide over the linoleum kitchen floor. They sniff* **TERESA**, *and* **TERESA** *hates this – no one moves.*)
>
> (*Later.*)

(**AUNT BOBBI, TERESA,** *and* **ROHIT** *are together.*)

(**TERESA** *doesn't look at* **ROHIT.**)

TERESA. The police came to the house at like eleven in the morning and my first thought was: *wrong house.* I had no sense of dread. And I opened the door and they asked if I was Winn and I lied and I said yes, I said I was Winn. And this was just – I just have a terrible lying compulsion tbh. And they asked me if I knew Asher Lowden and I said...the...*country singer*? And they said, they were just like: do you *personally* know anyone by that name?

AUNT BOBBI. Were they from the sheriff's office?

TERESA. I don't know they were extraordinarily cop-y people, just absolute literal police, and I – but maybe? And then I said I wasn't really Winn. Then Winn came out and left with them and I threw up.

ROHIT. You had no idea she was, is my

TERESA. Obviously my first thought was: did Winn murder the famous early-aughts country singer Asher Lowden?

AUNT BOBBI. Your first thought was *of course* she / *what*?

TERESA. / Of course!

ROHIT. / You thought that Winn murdered Asher Lowden?

AUNT BOBBI. What on earth is wrong with you? What in the heck / is wrong with you?

TERESA. I don't even watch that many crime shows, but I guess I've seen enough to. / Yeah.

AUNT BOBBI. That's just too entirely crazy.

TERESA. It was just my first thought, which I actually think is a perfectly reasonable first thought. I've never liked someone I thought would be literally incapable of murder.

AUNT BOBBI. Wow, you are really, really crazy.

TERESA. Sure but after a minute or whatever, I felt differently, and it was worse! I – and by the way I was actually *with* her when he died, so also she didn't kill him, if that's / what you're thinking.

AUNT BOBBI. / Yeah, we weren't thinking that.

ROHIT. Certainly was not thinking that.

TERESA. I assumed he was dead since they came up to the house and asked if I knew him but. I didn't even know what to suffer about, and I also knew that something was so wrong, irreversibly? A horrible feeling: something is irreversibly wrong. And even worse: I don't know what it is.

ROHIT. Yeah. I get that.

TERESA. And then she got home.

AUNT BOBBI. Did Winn know who he was?

TERESA. What do you mean.

AUNT BOBBI. Did she know he was a famous guy when she met him or did she just think: here's a guy.

TERESA. I don't know. I don't know what she thought.

TERESA. She got home and she said that Asher Lowden had been in a car accident. And that he had been drunk and it was unclear how on-purpose the – if it had been on purpose. And like: he died. And so they looked through his stuff and the last person he had texted was Winn. And I said okay: why was he texting you? And she said I have been having sex with him for about five weeks and I said for some reason something like *this is going to be annoying*. Instead of – like I didn't say anything nice at all. I had...like...nothing...nice to say to her. And I said I am sure you want comfort and I'm unfortunately not the person who can give that to you today. And she said I'm going to go to Aunt Bobbi's house and then – so this – I was like – I was being really crazy and I said: No. *I'm* going to Aunt Bobbi's house. And she was like: okay.

ROHIT. But you had never been here before?

TERESA. The next morning, this morning. *This morning?* This morning. We thought we might as well like both go? *And* by the way I *do think* she is very in love with me. But before we left she called Em. So then. So I drove myself.

(**ROHIT** *yells or something.*)

ROHIT. WHAT happened.

TERESA. / What are you

AUNT BOBBI. / Probably a wasp.

ROHIT. That HURT wow that HURT oh my god that HURT.

(**ROHIT** *screams at a wasp.*)

FUCK YOU SERIOUSLY FUCK YOU WHAT THE FUCK OH MY GOD FUCK YOU.

I can't believe how much that hurt.

TERESA. I'm sorry.

AUNT BOBBI. They're pretty bad out here.

TERESA. Want me to get you some ice?

ROHIT. No.

(**TERESA** *looks at* **ROHIT.**)

TERESA. Do you want to see if I have a healing touch?

ROHIT. Ah. Okay.

(**TERESA** *touches* **ROHIT.**)

(*It's kind of working?*)

ROHIT. Oh it's kind of –

Working?

TERESA. I thought it might.

> (**AUNT BOBBI** *doesn't like any of this.*)

AUNT BOBBI. Okay then, well I'm gonna go let the dogs out in the front.

> (**AUNT BOBBI** *sort of leaves.*)

> (**TERESA** *gives their healing touch to* **ROHIT** *for a long time.*)

> (*They hear gunshots.*)

TERESA. Are those gunshots?

ROHIT. Yeah they're shooting armadillos?

TERESA. Why are there armadillos?

ROHIT. Uh I assume? Climate? Catastrophe?

TERESA. Sad.

ROHIT. I want to say something inappropriate.

TERESA. Are you attracted to me?

ROHIT. Oh. I was going to say um I. I wondered if you knew that Em and Winn were like...girlfriends in college.

TERESA. *Girlfriends?*

ROHIT. Or whatever / you call it.

TERESA. Yeah I knew they were girlfriends.

ROHIT. Okay I just wanted to make sure you knew that.

TERESA. Did Em break up with you for Winn at some point?

ROHIT. Yeah.

TERESA. *(Sympathetic.)* Yeah.

I'm going to take my hand off of you.

(They do.)

Do you feel better?

ROHIT. Oh. Ah. Yeah.

TERESA. Do you want a little bit of Ketamine?

ROHIT. I should not.

TERESA. You'll be fine. You'll acclimate.

ROHIT. To what?

*(**TERESA** shrugs.)*

(Everyone is together.)

> (**AUNT BOBBI** *talks to* **WINN** *and* **EM** *as if* **ROHIT** *and* **TERESA** *aren't there.*)

AUNT BOBBI. How much money do you have in your bank account.

EM. Why? / Oh.

AUNT BOBBI. Winn.

WINN. Me? / Um.

AUNT BOBBI. What's wrong with asking that? I don't understand what's wrong with asking that. I get the feeling she's broke.

WINN. Yeah.

AUNT BOBBI. Was he giving you money? The guy?

WINN. No.

EM. Why would he / have done that?

AUNT BOBBI. Yeah, well. Too bad. How much do you have in your / checking account.

WINN. I really don't want to tell you that.

EM. Aunt Bobbi let's let Winn take a nap or let's not make her / think.

AUNT BOBBI. Well I'm gonna give you fifty dollars. Are you gonna go to the funeral?

> (**WINN** *shakes her head, no.*)

Yeah I guess not, cus'a the. Have you ever met the wife?

> (**WINN** *nods.*)

WINN. Just. At the. After.

AUNT BOBBI. Yeah I feel pretty bad for her.

EM. Oh my god.

AUNT BOBBI. He was too old for you.

EM. Who cares?

AUNT BOBBI. Was it a suicide?

EM. Aunt Bobbi, oh my god.

AUNT BOBBI. What's the problem I'm sorry I'm just asking the questions: how are you feeling?

> (**WINN** *shakes her head like she's trying to say: "I'm not going to tell you." But maybe, she accidentally loses it. Maybe she almost can't say, or is inaudible when she says:*)

WINN. Heartbroken?

> (**AUNT BOBBI** *hugs* **WINN**. *Big hug. Maybe it goes on a while.*)

> (**WINN** *tries to get it together. Maybe* **AUNT BOBBI** *keeps her in a hug.*)

AUNT BOBBI. Did you love him?

WINN. No. No.

AUNT BOBBI. Just a little scary?

WINN. Yeah.

AUNT BOBBI. Just freakin' sad?

WINN. Yeah.

AUNT BOBBI. It's definitely not your fault, okay?

Okay?

WINN. Okay.

> (**AUNT BOBBI** *makes some kind of adjustment,*
> *looks at* **EM.***)*

AUNT BOBBI. Did you know about this?

EM. Uh. No.

AUNT BOBBI. Huh. Interesting.

> *(A little bit later.)*

> (**WINN** *is sleeping.* **AUNT BOBBI** *is doing*
> *something with the dogs.)*

> (**ROHIT** *is in a room.* **TERESA** *is in another.)*

> (**EM** *gets too close to* **WINN.** *Maybe "wakes her*
> *up," aggressively "whispers":)*

EM. I'm gonna sleep in here with you.

WINN. Okay.

EM. How are you feeling?

WINN. I don't know.

EM. They were talking about you on NPR.

WINN. Are you okay?

EM. Yeah? What? Yes. Who cares.

WINN. What have you been doing.

EM. I was vaping in the yard for so long I was hoping I could get my eyes to bleed.

WINN. What's wrong?

EM. Shut up nothing.

They took Melba offline.

WINN. I'm so sorry.

EM. They said it was for ethical problems.

WINN. I'm so sorry.

EM. I loved her for her ethical problems.

WINN. Yeah.

EM. But now you're here and like you're the.

WINN. Yeah but that doesn't matter.

EM. Yeah. Never leave me.

(**WINN** *thinks this is funny but also annoying.*)

WINN. Whatever.

(*It's only a little bit later. Everyone is together. Everyone is explaining "the situation" to* **AUNT BOBBI.***)*

> *(Maybe **WINN** is just entering this heated moment; maybe she's been in bed the whole time until now.)*

AUNT BOBBI. They find his car at his work, but they can't find him?

ROHIT. He probably never left the parking lot.

EM. / He did. They have the fucking footage.

WINN. / Are you talking about Stanley Chi?

ROHIT. / *(Quiet, re: **EM**'s tone.)* Wow, okay.

> *(No one looks at **WINN** or answers her. She scans the room desperately for eye contact for a moment –)*

EM. He left the thing exactly when his friend said he left.

TERESA. The cops didn't believe her / because she was a

WINN. They thought she was wrong.

EM. I wouldn't have believed her. She is that classic type.

TERESA. The coworker is a classic type?

EM. Winn had a phase of being like that.

WINN. Being like what.

EM. Like pretentiously homely clothes and mentally ill hair.

> *(**WINN** thinks this is hilarious. **TERESA** really, really does not.)*

TERESA. Mentally? / Ill? Hair?

EM. There's footage of him leaving the restaurant when he said he was taking a cigarette break. And then he came back. At seven a.m.

WINN. And no one knows where he went in the meantime.

EM. Well they know he went to the Shell Station.

WINN. / They do?

TERESA. There's a video at the Shell Station.

WINN. / *(To* **TERESA.***)* I didn't even know you were following it.

(**TERESA** *does not acknowledge* **WINN.***)*

TERESA. He looks normal.

EM. He buys like a giant energy drink or something. / Disgusting.

TERESA. He actually gets the cigarettes.

EM. And then he drives somewhere but he doesn't get back to the restaurant until seven in the morning.

AUNT BOBBI. He got out of the car?

EM. He gets out of the car but you can't see where he goes.

TERESA. Jumped off a bridge.

ROHIT. Is there a bridge?

TERESA. I just can't think of another place he would go.

ROHIT. / Than a bridge?

TERESA. Like he's dead obviously somewhere.

AUNT BOBBI. Now was there something wrong with him?

EM. Not noticeably / but probably.

AUNT BOBBI. Everybody's sick in the head. Cora Waterman said he did drugs.

EM. Everybody does drugs.

AUNT BOBBI. That's kinda what I mean.

WINN. Not everybody / does drugs.

EM. Is it like our fault because we never let him be friends
with us?

TERESA. I didn't know that happened.

WINN. I was friends with him. I wasn't – I didn't –

EM. Rohit and I weren't that nice to him.

ROHIT. I was nice to him! We spent a whole semester
making Mesopotamia! It was / really really good!

EM. This is – yeah – this is what I worried about because I
think it's my fault.

WINN. / There's no way it has to...

EM. Wait wait wait – do they have his phone?

WINN. Maybe it's locked.

AUNT BOBBI. How did they get into Asher Lowden's phone?

WINN. They um. They didn't. The police didn't actually.

TERESA. / Yes they did.

AUNT BOBBI. *(To* **WINN.***)* Oh lord, oh right, so you were
the last / person he called.

WINN. / They didn't. The police didn't get into it.

EM. / I don't get it.

WINN. The police didn't get into it. They called his wife,
and she went to the hospital. He actually died at the
hospital.

AUNT BOBBI. Now so how exactly did he die? / Blood loss?
Bleeding?

TERESA. And she went through his phone?

(**WINN** *nods.*)

WINN. She had to use his dead face.

ROHIT. I don't think that would work, / actually.

WINN. *(To* **AUNT BOBBI.***)* He accelerated into one of those ruptured pieces of pavement? I? They think? His car flew out – he hit – head injuries.

AUNT BOBBI. So that's gruesome. / An accident, right?

TERESA. The wife found your texts?

ROHIT. / I think the face…

WINN. Yeah. She asked the police to find me. As like. A favor.

ROHIT. Because there wasn't a crime.

TERESA. Well if he had lived, he would've gotten a DUI.

WINN. It wasn't a criminal investigation. She just wanted to know if. I don't know. If I knew something. And she's like. Friends with the cops.

AUNT BOBBI. Did you talk to her?

TERESA. / Are they allowed to do that?

EM. That's actually fucked up.

TERESA. Yeah I'm sorry. That's actually fucked up.

EM. Was he a Republican?

AUNT BOBBI. Stanley Chi?

EM. No, Asher Lowden.

TERESA. Don't say something gross.

WINN. Wait what. What's / gross?

TERESA. Like that you didn't *talk much* or

WINN. We talked actually. We talked a lot / actually.

TERESA. Oh okay that's worse.

EM. Was he a Sagittarius?

> (**WINN** *actually thinks this is hilarious,* *nods: yep.)*

> (**EM** *thinks this hilarious too. Everyone else* *hates this.)*

AUNT BOBBI. I don't understand these people and I don't want to.

> (**AUNT BOBBI** *regards* **EM** *with disgust.)*

> (*It's a little bit later. Maybe it's even the next* *night. Everyone is together.)*

> (*They are playing charades.)*

> (*It's possible that there is suddenly a sense* *that they are performing for us, that they are* *actually trying to get us to guess what the* *clues are.)*

> (**EM** *is acting out* Sharp Objects.*)*

> (*She tries to enact plying out teeth.)*

WINN. *The Argonauts?*

TERESA. How did you...what? / Why did you –

WINN. I don't know, I'm just guessing something I think you would've written down.

TERESA. *(So upset.)* That is not how the game *works!*

> (**EM** *acts out cutting something with scissors.)*

WINN. *Ulysses*

TERESA. / Oh my god.

ROHIT. / What?

WINN. *Care Bears*!

TERESA. / You can't play it like that!

AUNT BOBBI. Cutting. Cutting the what. / Cutting the what.

WINN. *Edward Scissorhands*! *Edward Scissorhands*!

(**EM** *acts out cutting herself.*)

Um – Sylvia...Plath.

EM. This one / is too hard.

TERESA. / No talking! Wait let me see what it is.

ROHIT. Did she *cut* herself?

WINN. *In the Dream House.* Um. Um. *Conflict is not Abuse.* / Wait. Can't we ask like

EM. This is too hard this is too hard I'm getting a new one.

TERESA. *(Outraged.)* What do you mean. You can't just. *(They hate themselves, whisper.)* Pick a new one.

(**EM** *somehow "picks a new one." It's* The Argonauts.)

(**EM** *points furiously at* **WINN.**)

WINN. Me? Um.

(**EM** *nods.*)

TERESA. No nodding!

(**EM** *gestures frantically at* **WINN.**)

WINN. Oh! Um – my – oh it's a book. Is it / a book?

EM. Book. Yes.

WINN. / *Things Fall Apart.*

TERESA. No talking!

(**EM** *gestures, somehow more frantically at* **WINN**.)

WINN. *My Brilliant Friend.*

(**EM** *makes a "keep going" gesture...*)

Um – ah what's the second one ah – *The Story of the Lost Child...*

(**EM** *groans.*)

TERESA. Time's up times up.

WINN. I'm sorry I'm horrible.

EM. Ah! That one actually was *The Argonauts.*

(*This is hysterical to them [not to* **TERESA** *].*)

TERESA. Oh my god I hate myself / I actually hate myself.

AUNT BOBBI. I don't know what / half this crap is.

ROHIT. I'm going.

(**ROHIT** *gets* A Wrinkle in Time.*)*

(*He really considers for a bit.*)

(*He mimes "book."*)

AUNT BOBBI. / Book.

TERESA. Book.

(*He puts up three fingers.*)

AUNT BOBBI. Three words.

TERESA. *Song of Solomon.*

(He shakes his head and hands, corrects: Four fingers.)

AUNT BOBBI. / Four words.

TERESA. Four words. *Written on the Body*!

(He shakes his head.)

(He puts up four fingers again.)

Fourth word!

EM. I played / this wrong.

WINN. We're horrible.

EM. We don't know how to play this game I guess.

*(**ROHIT** mimes looking at a watch.)*

TERESA. Watch! Time!

*(**ROHIT** points at **TERESA**.)*

Fourth word *time*. Oh my god *The Order of Time The Order of Time The Order of Time*.

*(**ROHIT** puts up two fingers.)*

AUNT BOBBI. / Second word.

TERESA. Second word.

*(**ROHIT** mimes ironing.)*

EM. What are you, / a butler?

TERESA. Ironing. Iron. Iron out. Wrinkle *A Wrinkle in Time*!

ROHIT. Yep.

AUNT BOBBI. This one says she hates games okay I'm going. Everyone guesses.

TERESA. Wait but.

(*It's not* **AUNT BOBBI***'s turn. No one cares or even notices except for* **TERESA***.*)

Okay okay.

(**AUNT BOBBI** *"picks one."*)

AUNT BOBBI. Okay I don't know what the heck that is. Oh wait Cora Waterman's calling me. Hold on.

(*Everyone waits.*)

(*No one moves.*)

(**AUNT BOBBI** *looks somewhere, like she's talking to someone ten yards away.*)

(*It's weirdly loud. Maybe it's weirdly fast.*)

Hey, Cora. That's what I figured. I guess that's what everyone figured. So where was he? So was that... Oh well that's a nightmare and a half. When was that? How was that? Well now that's just gonna make everybody go crazy. Good thing everyone's already mentally ill. Did you talk to Ying? Did you talk to Joe? Did you talk to Bean? Is that not how you say it? Did you talk to Wendy? Did you talk to Jasmine? No the kids haven't heard yet because they don't call each other. Okay, well, say hi to everybody and Ying and Joe have the same address so I'm gonna send them the lasagna. Well that's a sure thing. Do you think she's gonna skip book club? Yeah we'll have to see, okay bye.

Well somebody from work found Stanley Chi inside of there.

EM. / What?

ROHIT. Inside the restaurant?

AUNT BOBBI. I guess he hung himself in a storage closet in the basement.

TERESA. Didn't they have a problem with like…the smell?

EM. It's been like / weeks.

WINN. Oh my god.

AUNT BOBBI. The whole thing of it seems pretty messed up. I guess because they also had some rotten meat in the walk-in and they thought it was that for a while and then it went away. And then I guess they just don't use the storage closet very much.

TERESA. Why did he do that at *work*?

EM. *(To* **AUNT BOBBI.***)* I'm sorry.

AUNT BOBBI. Okay, well the one I got was something I never heard of and was also too freakin' hard and I wasn't gonna act it out. So I'm gonna pick another one.

> *(***AUNT BOBBI*** *picks another one. It's like she's going to enact another charade title, but instead – She speaks to us.)*

You don't have to play games at the Grief Hotel if you don't want, but the games are bespoke. Same with the stretching class. It just is made for you in particular to feel good. Uh. You can make a list of things you're grateful about which is a really good one, so I like to picture something I'm grateful for which is easy for me it's dogs. Particularly my dogs but I can effectively zoom out and think well it was some kinda luck that was either magic or scientific that put me on a planet where dogs evolved and I can even invite them into my house. I have a lot of gratitude for that. I can even feed them. All that.

> *(***AUNT BOBBI*** *might have a microphone?)*

AUNT BOBBI. I'll go first with some gratitude. Mine today is: I'm grateful for dogs. Well – so – I'm grateful that I get to have pets and that mine are dogs. And so I could say in order to be inclusive that I'm grateful for pets. Well let's not go too far, ah; I'm grateful for dogs and cats. I'm grateful that we can live inside with smaller animals. Ah. Okay, that's mine. I'm grateful we can live inside with smaller animals. Okay so you do it with me.

> *(Ideally, the audience believes this includes them. If not, she still says this as if everyone is speaking with her.)*

> *(At the very least, **WINN**, **TERESA**, **EM** and **ROHIT** join her.)*

EVERYONE. I'm grateful we can live inside with smaller animals. I'm grateful we can live inside with smaller animals. I'm grateful we can live inside with smaller animals. I'm grateful we can live inside with smaller animals. I'm grateful we can live inside with smaller animals.

> *(**AUNT BOBBI** makes a gesture like she's cuing someone, but maybe it's that she's hearing something –)*

> *(She's hearing a nostalgic karaoke track.)*

> *(Maybe **AUNT BOBBI** is imagining the karaoke track, or summoning it, or hearing it from the room next door, which is exactly the way she'd like to experience it.)*

> *(If there were a karaoke machine, it would say:)*

> *("Roads Go" in the style of Asher Lowden, 2002.)*

> *(**AUNT BOBBI** speaks over the introduction.)*

AUNT BOBBI. At a certain point, everything bad that happens reminds you of something bad that has already happened so. I don't feel any need to tell you what makes my problems different than anybody else's. But I assume – I assume about you – that you can understand. We all, I mean, pretty much everybody needs a week. Or two.

> (*Maybe* **WINN** *and* **EM** *start the song –)*

> (*Maybe they appear, on mic, facing an invisible karaoke prompter; the dimensions change.)*

> (**EM** *cues* **WINN** *to start the song.)*

WINN.
> EVERYBODY KNOWING WHEN YOU LEFT AND WHEN YOU
> CAME
> CAN'T CUT LOOSE LIKE A HORSE ACROSS THE PLAIN

EM. *(Interrupts/shouts.)* LOUDER

WINN.
> WHISPER TO YOUR GIRL THAT YOU'RE NEVER COMING
> HOME

WINN & EM.
> CUS LORD ONLY KNOWS WHERE THE ROAD'S GONNA GO
> CUS LORD ONLY KNOWS WHERE THE ROAD'S GONNA GO
> (GO!)

> (**ROHIT** *and* **TERESA** *make something of the space. It's getting cozier, more complete –)*

> (*Maybe they hand* **AUNT BOBBI** *a gorgeous glass bowl of ethically-sourced sliced fruit. Maybe they bring her a robe. It fits her perfectly! Maybe the lapel is embroidered: "Aunt Bobbi." Maybe they present her room to*

> *her; the blankets are green and the view is the ocean.)*

EM.

EVERYBODY TELLS YOU THAT YOU NEED TO BEHAVE
STEP RIGHT STEP LEFT 'TIL YOU STEP INTO YOUR GRAVE
WHISPER TO YOUR GIRL THAT YOU'RE NEVER COMING
    HOME

WINN & EM.

CUS LORD ONLY KNOWS WHERE THE ROAD'S GONNA GO
LORD ONLY KNOWS WHERE THE ROAD'S GONNA GO (GO!)

> *(**EM** prompts **ROHIT** to sing!)*

ROHIT.

EVERYBODY MOVING LIKE THE WATER IN THE WELL
SPINNING ROUND AND ROUND AND DOWN THE DRAIN
    TO HELL
I DON'T KNOW WHO'S LEFT TO TELL YOU'RE NEVER
    COMIN' HOME

WINN, EM & ROHIT.

CUS LORD ONLY KNOWS WHERE THE ROAD'S GONNA GO
LORD ONLY KNOWS WHERE THE ROAD'S GONNA GO (GO!)

> *(Finally, **EM**, **WINN**, **ROHIT**, and **TERESA** are all part of the karaoke party – It's raucous and partially visible in the next room. They're really getting ahold of this nostalgic tune. They pass the mic.)*

> *(**EM** prompts **TERESA** to sing.)*

TERESA.

EVERYBODY KNOWING WHEN YOU LEFT AND WHEN YOU
    CAME
CAN'T CUT LOOSE LIKE A HORSE ACROSS THE PLAIN
WHISPER TO YOUR GIRL THAT YOU'RE NEVER COMING
    HOME

WINN, EM, ROHIT & TERESA.
CUS LORD ONLY KNOWS WHERE THE ROAD'S GONNA GO
LORD ONLY KNOWS WHERE THE ROAD'S GONNA GO (GO!)

(**AUNT BOBBI**'s *presentation becomes or continues to be her fantasy. She is the Grief Hotel, but she is also checked into the Grief Hotel.*)

(*Somehow, a transformation is complete.* **AUNT BOBBI** *has gifted us her vision. We're here! The karaoke is all-consuming. They jump and scream.*)

WINN, EM, ROHIT & TERESA.
EVERYBODY TELLS YOU THAT YOU NEED TO BEHAVE.
STEP RIGHT, STEP LEFT, AND STEP INTO YOUR GRAVE.

(**EM** *shuts everyone else up, insists that* **WINN** *take this next line:*)

WINN.
WHISPER TO YOUR GIRL THAT YOU'RE NEVER COMING
HOME

WINN, EM, ROHIT & TERESA.
CUS LORD ONLY KNOWS WHERE THE ROAD'S GONNA GO
LORD ONLY KNOWS WHERE THE ROAD'S GONNA GO (GO)

AUNT BOBBI. Welcome.